490L

12/2021

Dear Parents:

Congratulations! Your child is taking the first steps on an exciting journey. The destination? Independent reading!

STEP INTO READING® will help your child get there. The program offers five steps to reading success. Each step includes fun stories and colorful art or photographs. In addition to original fiction and books with favorite characters, there are Step into Reading Non-Fiction Readers, Phonics Readers and Boxed Sets, Sticker Readers, and Comic Readers—a complete literacy program with something to interest every child.

Learning to Read, Step by Step!

Ready to Read   Preschool–Kindergarten
• big type and easy words • rhyme and rhythm • picture clues
For children who know the alphabet and are eager to begin reading.

Reading with Help   Preschool–Grade 1
• basic vocabulary • short sentences • simple stories
For children who recognize familiar words and sound out new words with help.

Reading on Your Own   Grades 1–3
• engaging characters • easy-to-follow plots • popular topics
For children who are ready to read on their own.

Reading Paragraphs   Grades 2–3
• challenging vocabulary • short paragraphs • exciting stories
For newly independent readers who read simple sentences with confidence.

Ready for Chapters   Grades 2–4
• chapters • longer paragraphs • full-color art
For children who want to take the plunge into chapter books but still like colorful pictures.

STEP INTO READING® is designed to give every child a successful reading experience. The grade levels are only guides; children will progress through the steps at their own speed, developing confidence in their reading.

Remember, a lifetime love of reading starts with a single step!

Step into Reading, Random House, and the Random House colophon are registered trademarks of Penguin Random House LLC.

Visit us on the Web!
StepIntoReading.com
rhcbooks.com

Educators and librarians, for a variety of teaching tools, visit us at RHTeachersLibrarians.com

ISBN 978-0-7364-4237-4 (trade) — ISBN 978-0-7364-9006-1 (lib. bdg.)
ISBN 978-0-7364-4238-1 (ebook)

Printed in the United States of America   10 9 8 7 6 5 4 3 2 1

DISNEY
ENCANTO

Family is Everything

by Luz M. Mack

illustrated by the Disney Storybook Art Team

Random House 🏠 New York

This is Mirabel Madrigal.
She is kind and funny,
and she loves her family.

Her family lives
in a magical home
named Casita.

Mirabel has two
older sisters.
Luisa is strong.

Isabela can make flowers.

She is perfect.

She and Mirabel
do not get along.

Mirabel is the only one
who does not have
a magical gift.

Her mom worries
that she feels left out.
Mirabel is still special.

Abuela looks out
for the family
and the magic of Casita.

One night, Mirabel
overhears Abuela.
Abuela says the magic
of Casita is dying.

Bruno is Mirabel's uncle.

He can see the future.

He saw the magic dying.

Mirabel thinks Luisa
knows about
Bruno's vision.
But Luisa is upset.
Everyone wants her help.

Mirabel listens to Luisa.

Luisa feels better.

She tells Mirabel

to check Bruno's tower

for the missing vision.

Mirabel finds the pieces
of Bruno's vision.
She is at the center.

Mirabel finds Bruno
hiding inside Casita.
Bruno finishes his vision.
It shows her and Isabela!
Mirabel needs to
embrace her sister.

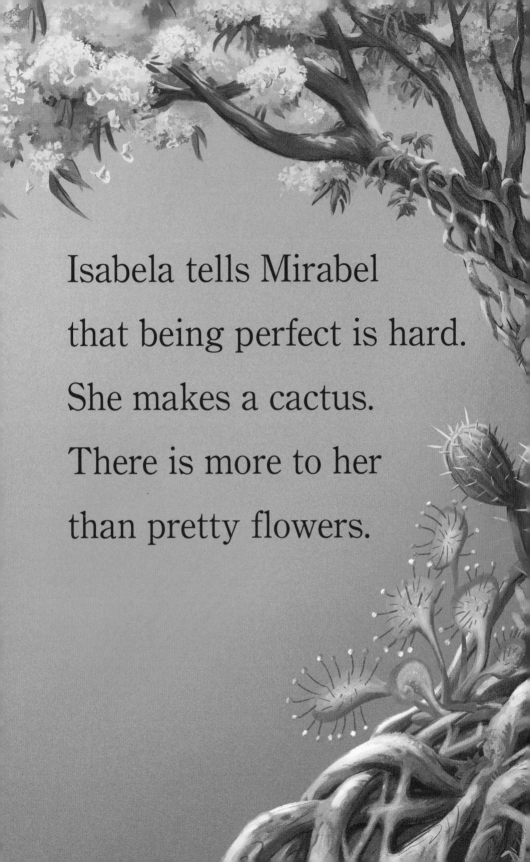

Isabela tells Mirabel
that being perfect is hard.
She makes a cactus.
There is more to her
than pretty flowers.

Casita cracks.
Abuela says Mirabel is
causing the magic to die.

But Mirabel says
it is Abuela's fault.

Abuela expects too much.

Casita falls apart.

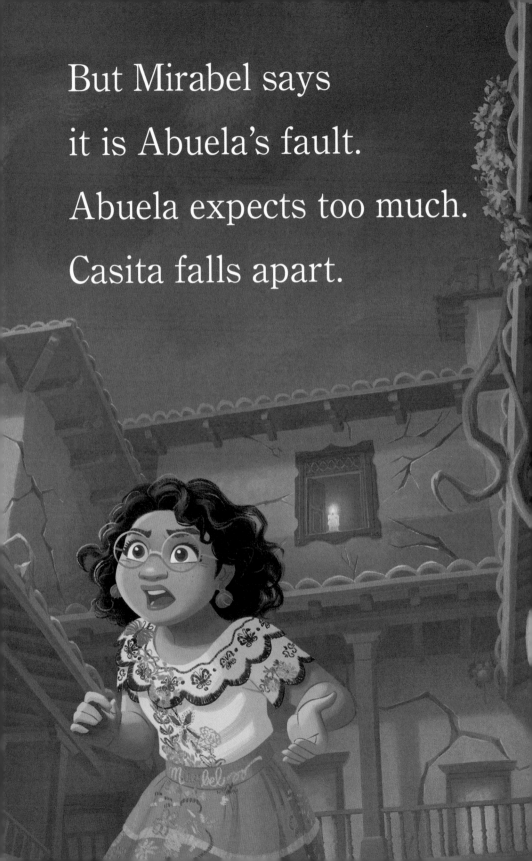

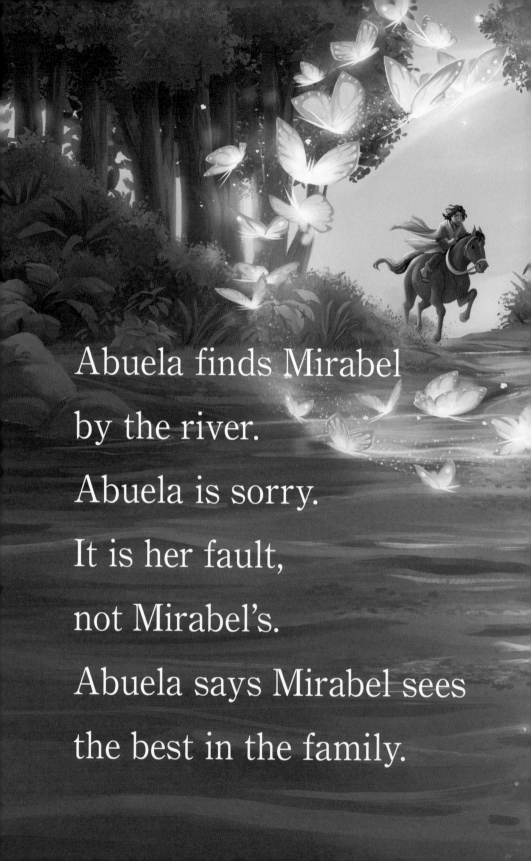

Abuela finds Mirabel
by the river.
Abuela is sorry.
It is her fault,
not Mirabel's.
Abuela says Mirabel sees
the best in the family.

They rebuild Casita.
The magic returns!
The family Madrigal
is closer than ever.